The Nian Monster

Andrea Wang

pictures by Alina Chau

Albert Whitman & Company
Chicago, Illinois

Three days before Chinese New Year, Shanghai was alive with color and sound.

Xingling and her grandmother hung the last of the decorations. "Po Po," Xingling asked, "Why are they all red? There is no blue, no pink, no purple."

"Long ago," Po Po said, "the Nian Monster lived in the mountains. His jaws were as wide as caverns. His teeth were sharper than swords. And he was filled with a terrible hunger. Each new year, Nian ate whole villages!"

Xingling gasped. "What happened to him?"
"Every monster has a weakness. Nian had three—loud sounds, fire, and the color red. Our traditions have kept Nian away ever since." Po Po smiled. "Now, I must go buy more noodles. Watch the casserole for me."

In the kitchen, Xingling lifted the lid and stirred the pot. The aroma of pork and cabbage wafted out the window.

Tong tong!

There on the balcony crouched a horrible beast. His jaws were as wide as caverns. His teeth were sharper than swords.

"*Ai ya!*" Xingling cried. "Nian has returned!"
"I have come to devour this city!" growled Nian.
He stretched his wide, wicked jaws and roared.
All the buildings in Shanghai shook.

Xingling pointed to the city below. "We have red banners!
Lanterns! Gongs and drums! Why aren't you scared?"

"*Pei!*" the monster spat. "That was thousands of years ago.
Those old tricks don't frighten me anymore. I am starving!"
He licked his lips. "You will make a tasty appetizer."

"Wait!" Xingling scanned the kitchen. "Have a bowl of long-life noodles first. If you live longer, you can conquer more cities."

Nian stroked one pointy horn. "You are wise, little one. Noodles first, then you, then the city."

"Good. Wait for me in the park."

Nian leaped down to People's Square and paced around the fountain.

Xingling ran to the best noodle shop in Shanghai. She asked the head chef to prepare a special dish just for Nian.

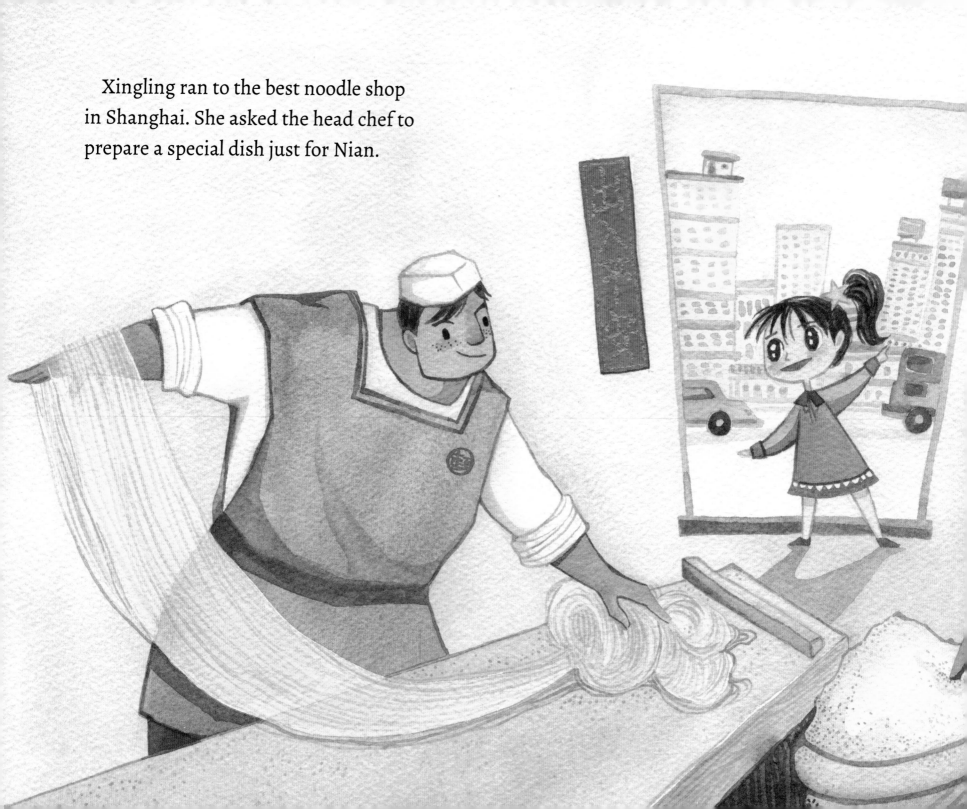

All day, the chefs mixed and kneaded and pulled. Finally, they pushed the giant bowl in front of Nian.

Nian slurped.
And slurped.
And slurped.

"My stomach is too stuffed to eat more," he groaned.
The chefs had made only one noodle. Just one! The longest noodle in China.
Nian belched. "I will devour the city tomorrow."

The next day, Nian glared down from the Jin Mao Tower and stretched his wide, wicked jaws.

"Wait!" Xingling yelled. "Eat fish first so you will have good fortune all year long."

Nian flicked his forked tail. "You are wise, little one. Fish first, then you, then the city."

"Good. Wait for me by the river."

Nian bounded over to the Oriental Pearl Tower and circled the largest globe.

Xingling ran to the best fishing fleet in Shanghai. She asked the captain to catch a special kind of fish just for Nian.

All day, the fishermen baited and hooked and scaled. Finally, they rowed the fish across the Huangpu River to Nian.

Nian gulped. And gulped. And gulped. The fish bones pricked and poked.

"My throat is too sore to eat more," he croaked.

The fishermen had caught only one kind of fish. Milkfish! The boniest fish in the sea.

Nian coughed. "I will devour the city tomorrow."

In the morning, Nian prowled through Yu Garden
and stretched his wide, wicked jaws.

"Wait!" said Xingling. "Tonight is New Year's Eve.
You need some rice cake to sweeten your future."

Nian gnashed his jagged teeth. "You are wise, little
one. Rice cake first, then you, then the city."

"Good. Wait for me at the teahouse."
Nian stalked across the zigzag bridge
to the Huxinting Teahouse.

Xingling ran home for the best rice cakes in Shanghai.
She asked Po Po to make a special rice cake just for Nian.

All day, the grandmothers stirred and steamed and fried. Finally, they rolled the enormous rice cake to Nian.

Nian chewed. And chewed. And chewed. The rice cake clung to his rows of sharp teeth.

Nian's wide, wicked jaws were stuck fast.

The grandmothers had used only glutinous rice flour. The stickiest kind! So sticky it had been used to build the Great Wall.

Nian rolled one monstrous yellow eye. "Rrrrrun mmuhmm unnhhh umgg," he muttered.

"Yes," Xingling said. "You can devour the city tomorrow. But first, fireworks! We must send out the old year so we can welcome in the new."

Xingling took Nian to the best place to see fireworks in Shanghai, the Bund.

She asked the fireworks master to put on a special show just for Nian. She gave Nian the seat of honor. "Sit here and watch."

Eight dancing dragons slid out from the crowd. They dipped and twisted and spun around Nian. At the midnight bell, the dragon dancers stopped and bowed.

The fireworks master held a match to the thick fuse.
"Good-bye, Old Year." Xingling waved. "Good-bye, Nian!"
Nian thrashed his mane and lashed his tail. But he couldn't
stretch those wide, wicked jaws to blow out the flame.

Pili pala! Nian and the chair blasted into the air.
The firework-makers had built a spectacular
firecracker. So spectacular it was a rocket!

Nian's claws tore a hole in the fabric of the sky. Just before he shot through, Nian shouted, "I'll be back next year!"

"Good," Xingling said. "You haven't tried my dumplings yet."

Author's Note

In the ancient legend, the Nian Monster woke once a year, at the Lunar New Year.

Ravenous, he devoured whole villages—the pigs, the cows, and the people! An old monk finally figured out how to scare Nian away. As Po Po says, the monster was afraid of the color red, loud noises, and fire. From then on, at Chinese New Year, people have decorated their houses with red banners and lanterns, beaten gongs and drums, and lit firecrackers to keep Nian away.

There are many foods traditionally eaten during New Year celebrations. The Lion's Head Casserole that attracts Nian to Xingling's apartment is a specialty of Shanghai. The large pork meatballs surrounded by napa cabbage are said to resemble a lion and its mane. Noodles are eaten to symbolize a long and happy life—the longer the better! Breaking a strand of long-life noodles is considered very unlucky.

Whole fish are often served at New Year and other big celebrations because the word for fish in Chinese, *yu*, sounds the same as the word for riches. Some people believe that eating fish will make your wishes come true in the new year.

Sticky rice cake symbolizes a rich, sweet life—but it won't really glue your jaws together! Chinese is a language full of homophones. The sound *nian* can either mean "year" or "sticky." In this story, the Nian Monster (the Year Monster) is defeated by *nian gao*, or sticky rice cake!

Other tasty Chinese tidbits:

- *Tong tong* is a Chinese onomatopoeia, or sound word, for "thud."
- *Ai ya* is a Chinese expression for "oh no" or "oh my goodness!"
- There are eight dancing dragons in the story because eight is the luckiest number in Chinese culture. Why? The word for eight, *ba*, rhymes with the word for good fortune, *fa*.
- Sticky rice flour really was used in the mortar to bind bricks together in the Great Wall. Six hundred years later, these sections of the wall are still standing!

For Tim, Evan, and Bennett, without whom no food
adventure would be complete—AW

I would like to dedicate this book to my family.—AC

Library of Congress Cataloging-in-Publication data is on file with the publisher.

Text copyright © 2016 by Andrea Wang
Pictures copyright © 2016 by Alina Chau
Published in 2016 by Albert Whitman & Company
ISBN 978-0-8075-5642-9

Printed in China
10 9 8 7 6 5 4 3 2 1 LP 24 23 22 21 20 19 18 17 16

Design by Jordan Kost

For more information about Albert Whitman & Company,
visit our web site at www.albertwhitman.com.